To all my friends, you are the colors of the rainbow
Para todos mis amigos y amigas,
ustedes son los colores del arcoíris
—R.C.L.

Text copyright © 2021 by René Colato Laínez
Illustrations copyright © 2021 by Nomar Perez
All Rights Reserved
HOLIDAY HOUSE is registered in the U.S. Patent and Trademark Office.
Printed and bound in August 2021 at C&C Offset, Shenzhen, China.
The artwork was created with digital tools.
www.holidayhouse.com
First Edition
1 3 5 7 9 10 8 6 4 2

Library of Congress Cataloging-in-Publication Data is available.
ISBN: 978-0-8234-4505-9 (hardcover)

MY FRIEND MI AMIGO

Let's Be Friends
Seamos Amigos

BY RENÉ COLATO LAÍNEZ   ILLUSTRATED BY NOMAR PEREZ

HOLIDAY HOUSE
NEW YORK

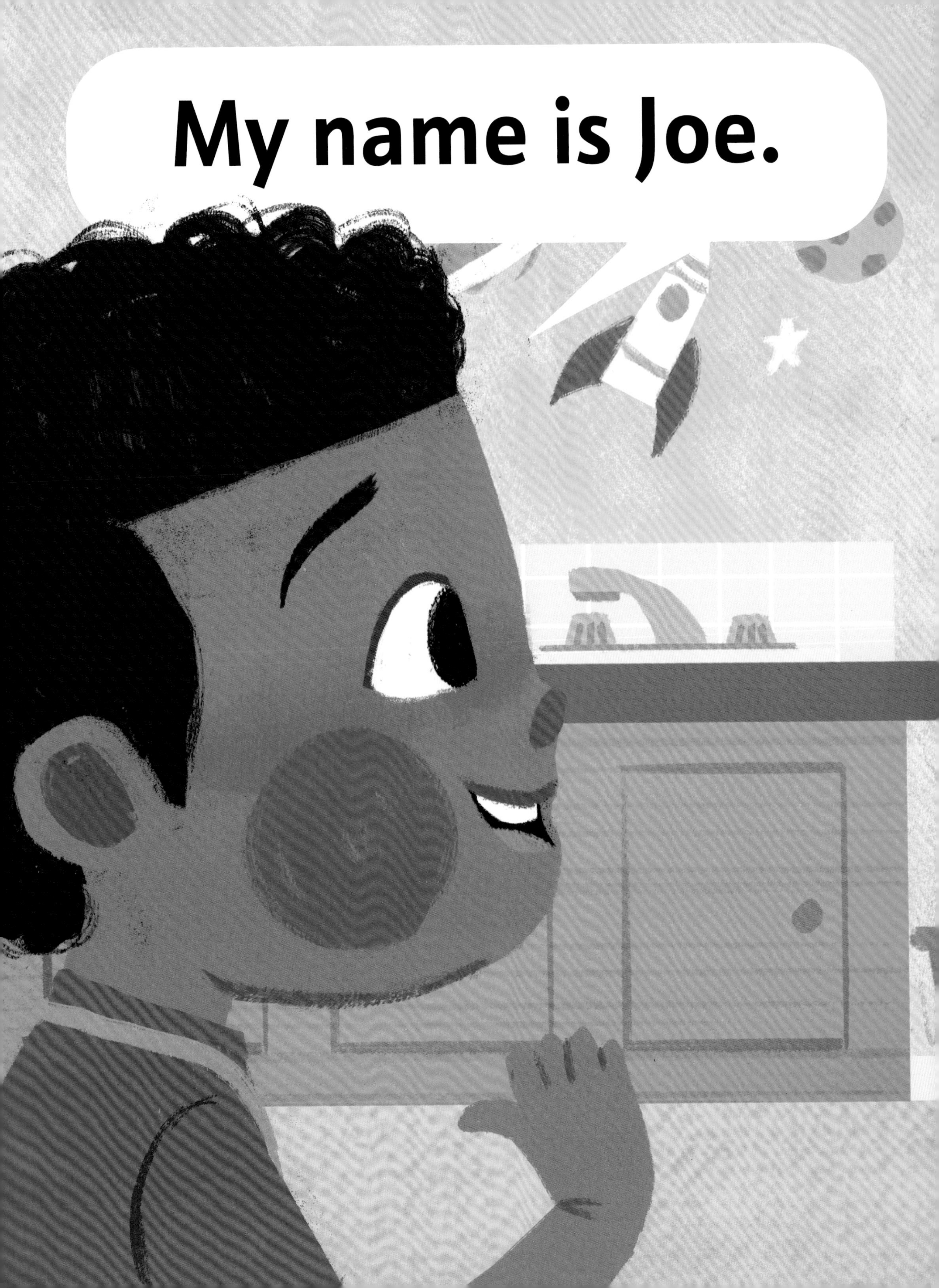
My name is Joe.

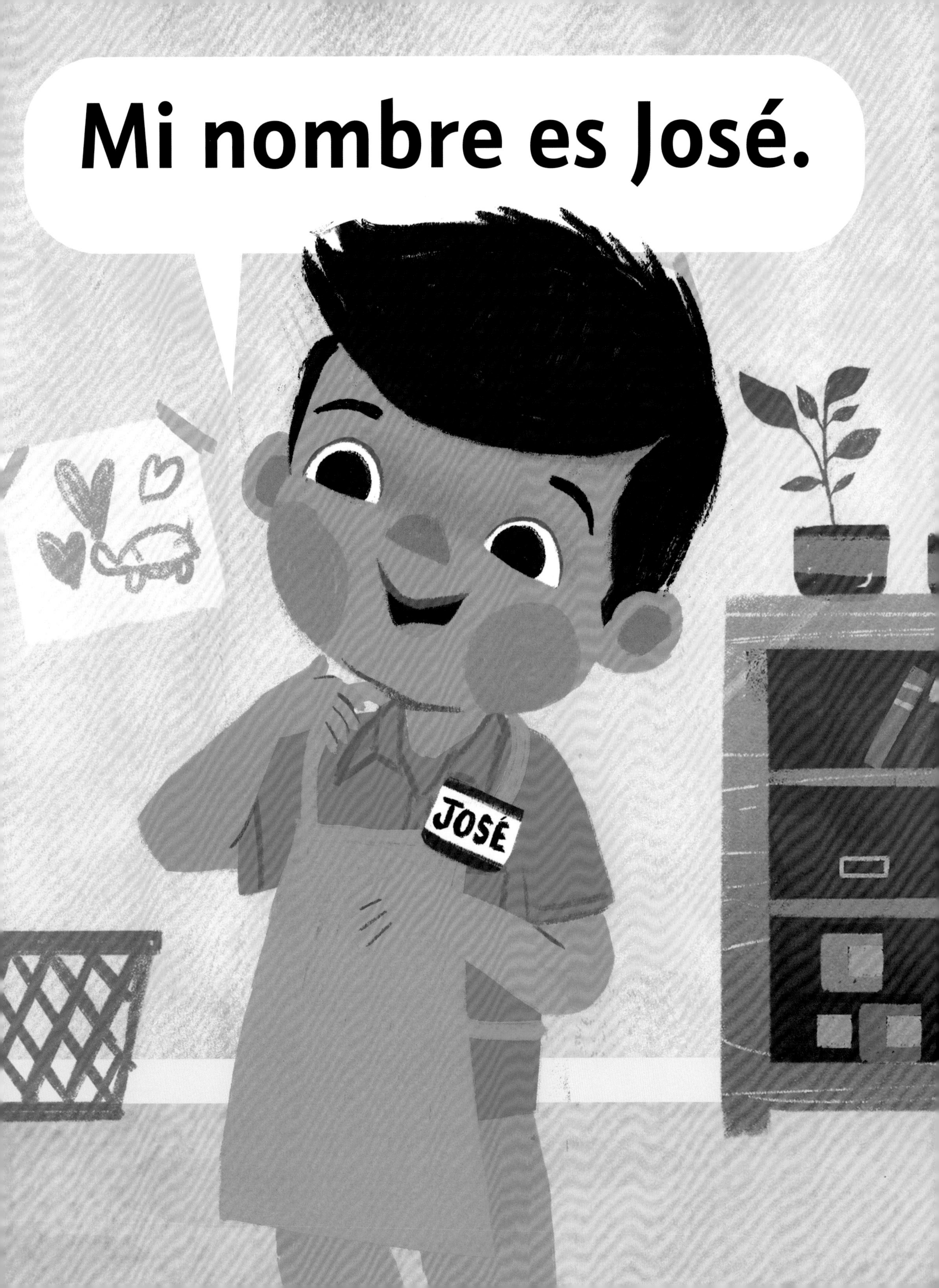
Mi nombre es José.
JOSÉ

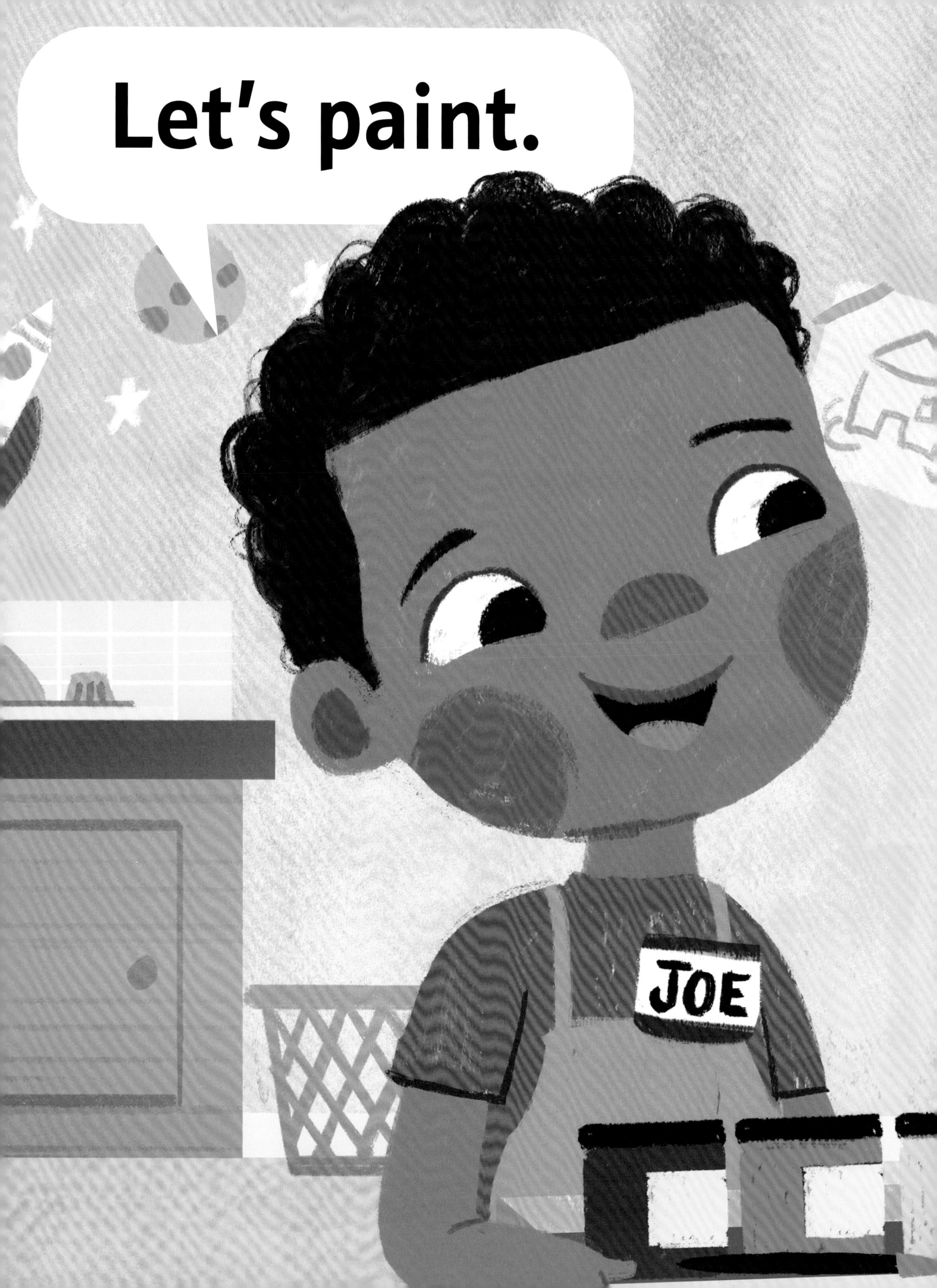
Let’s paint.
JOE

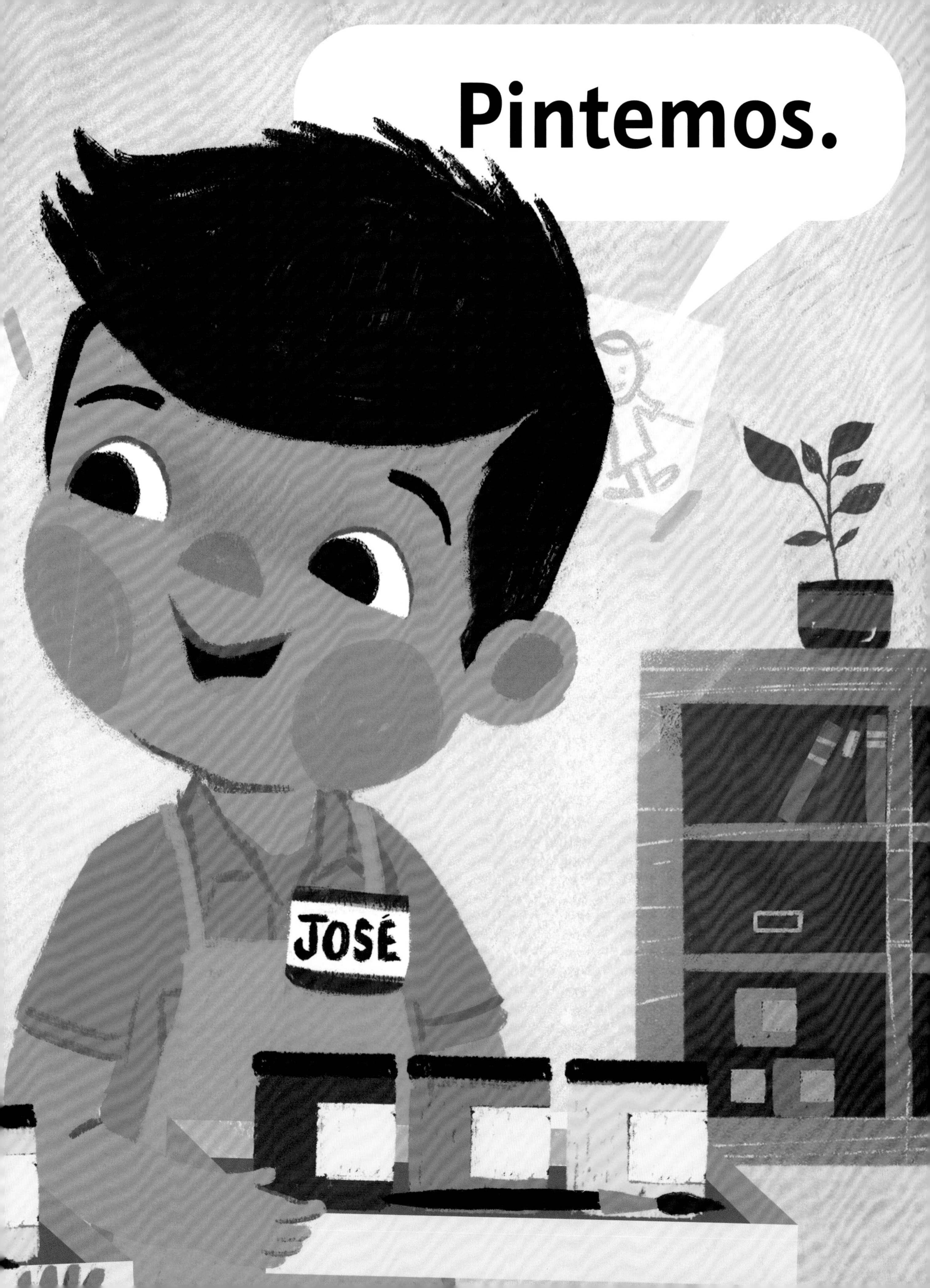
Pintemos.
JOSÉ

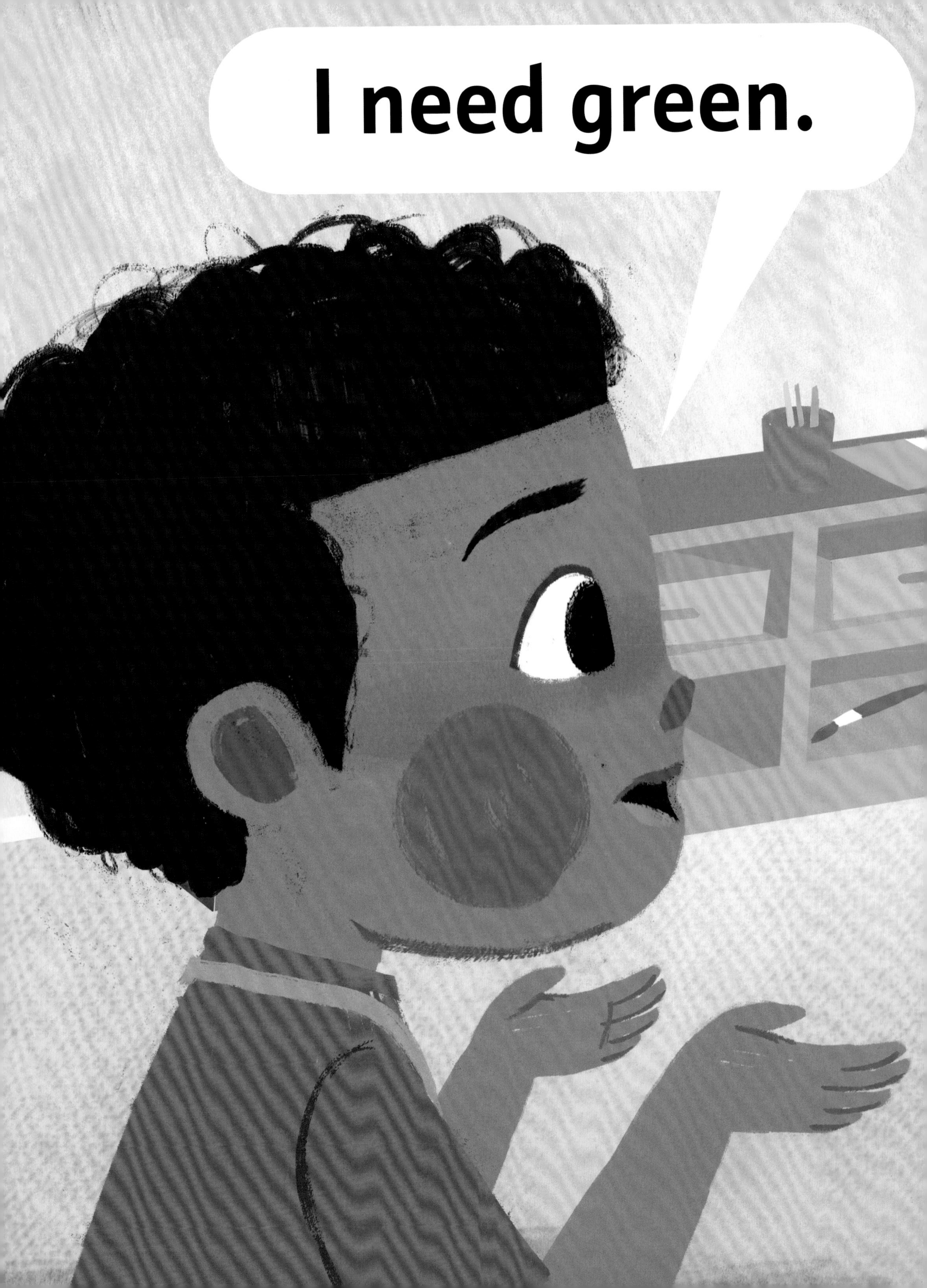
I need green.

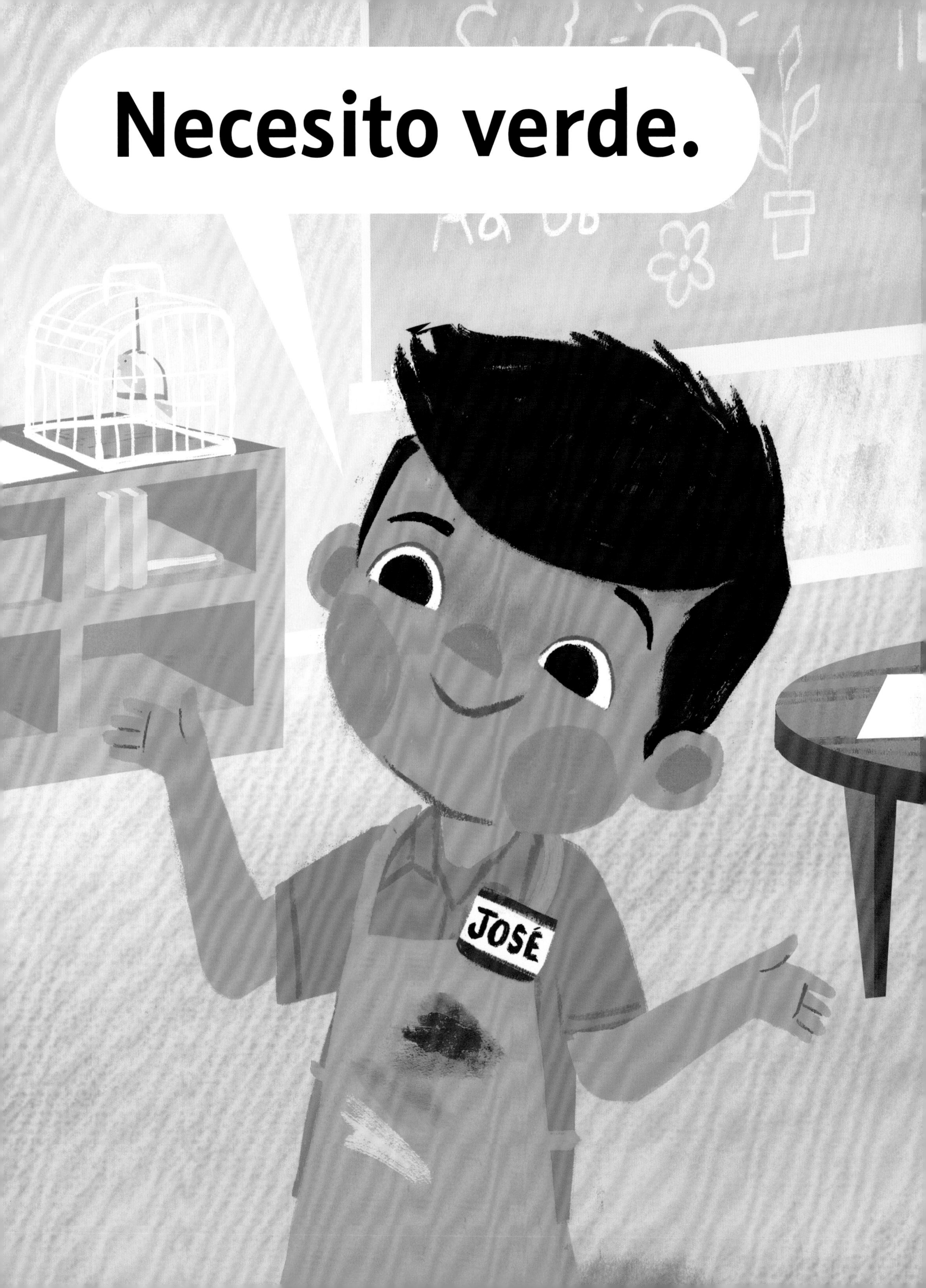
Necesito verde.
JOSÉ

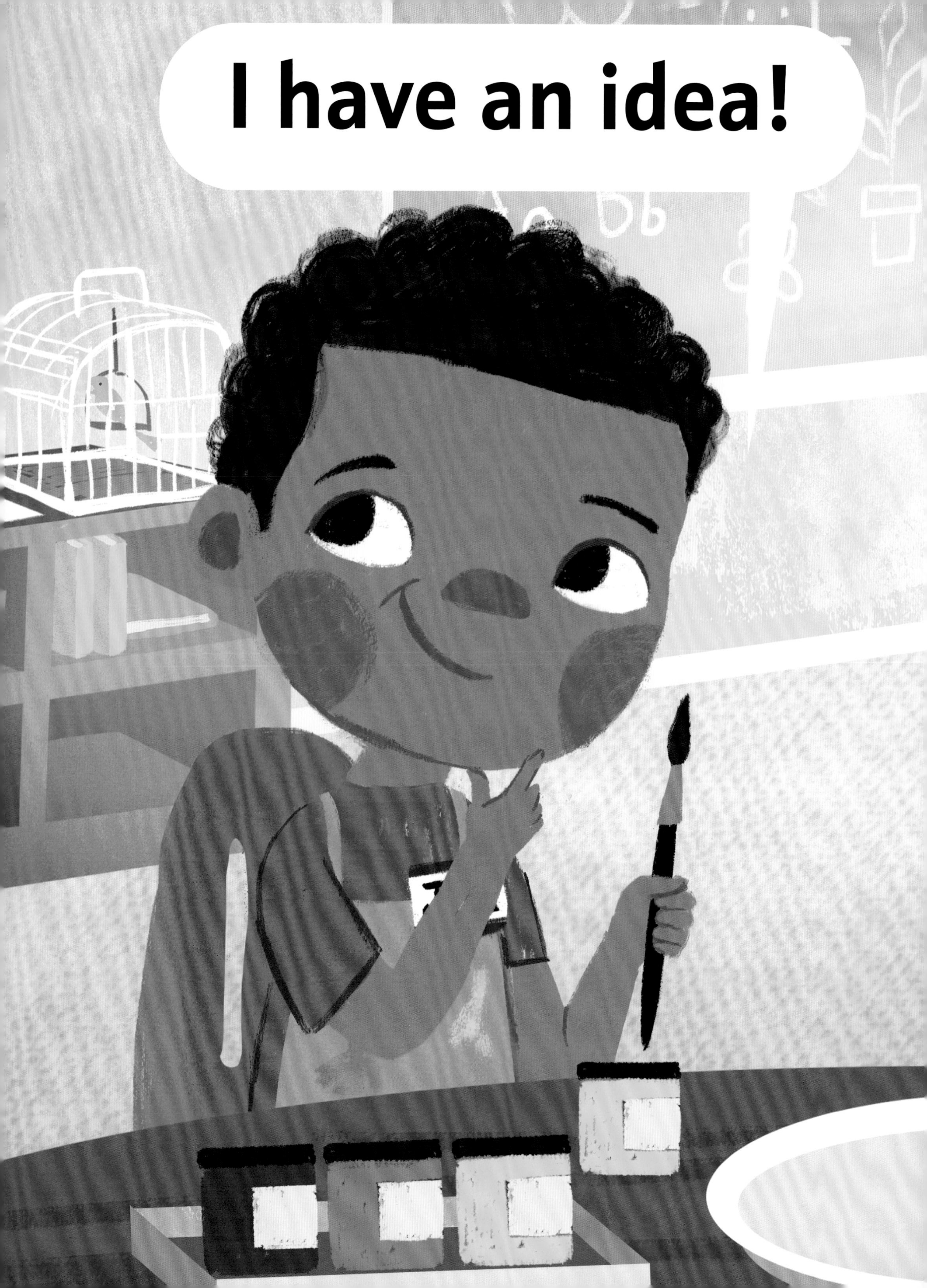
I have an idea!

Let's mix the colors.

Mezclemos los colores.

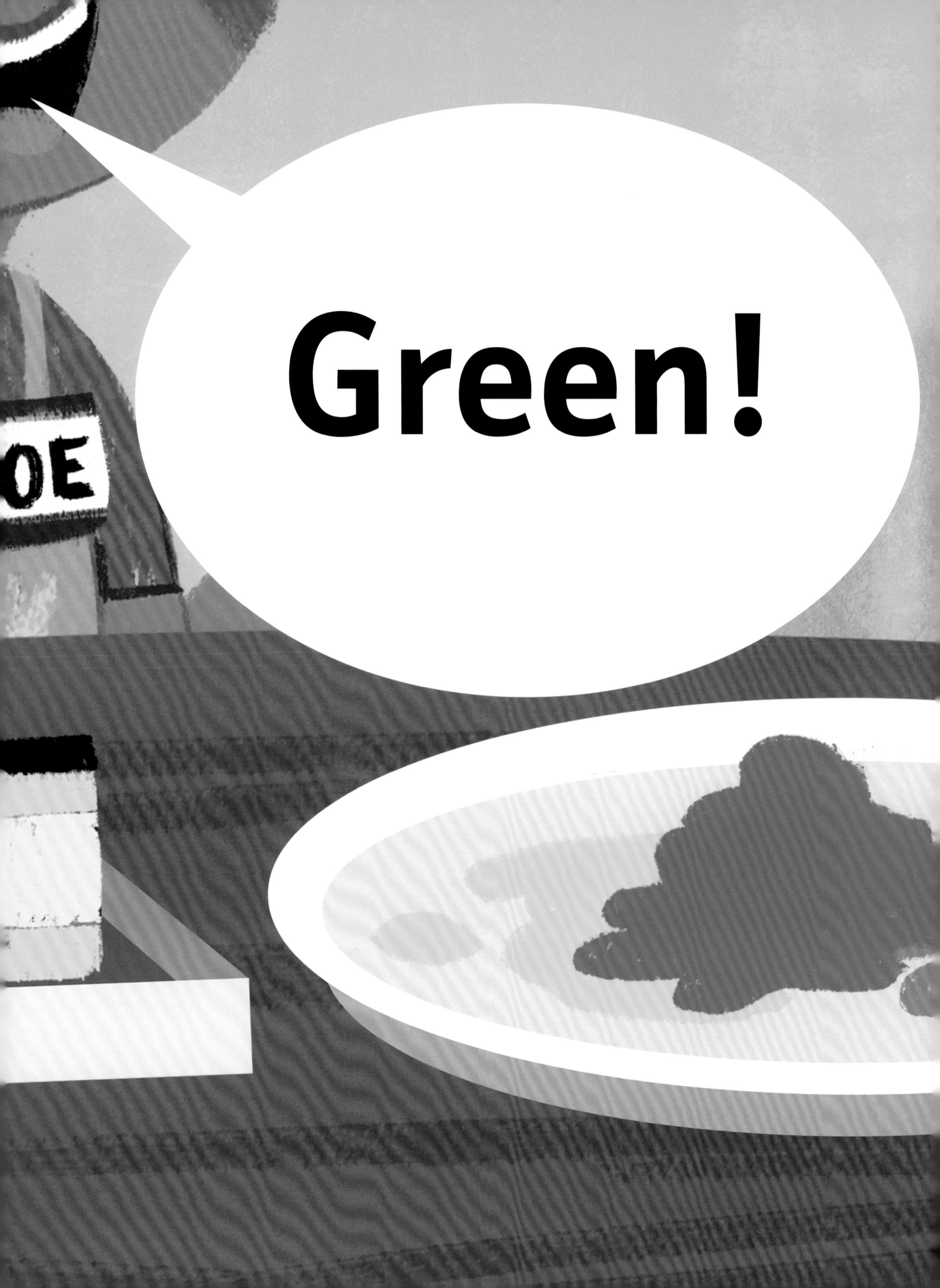
Green!
OE

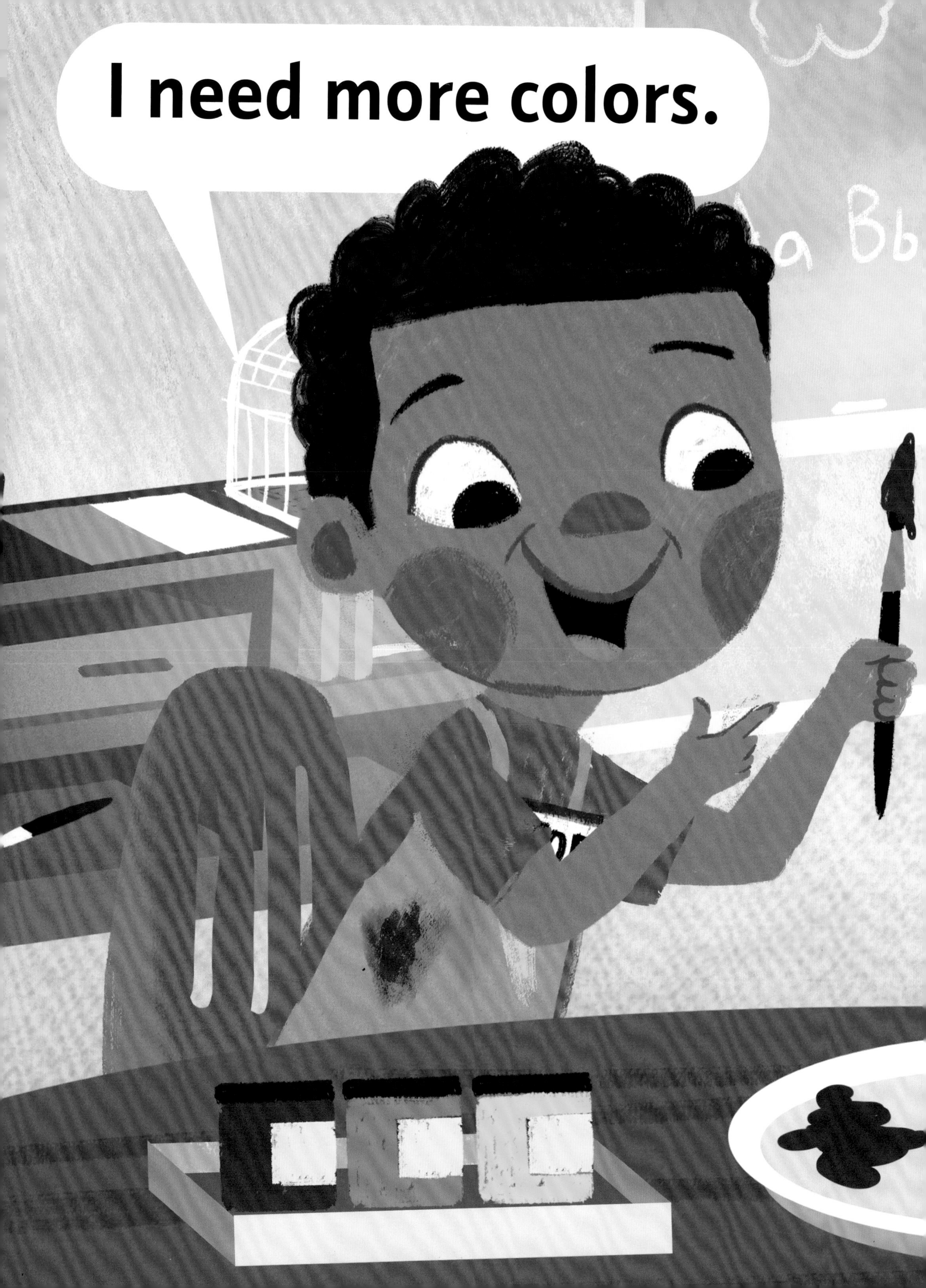
I need more colors.

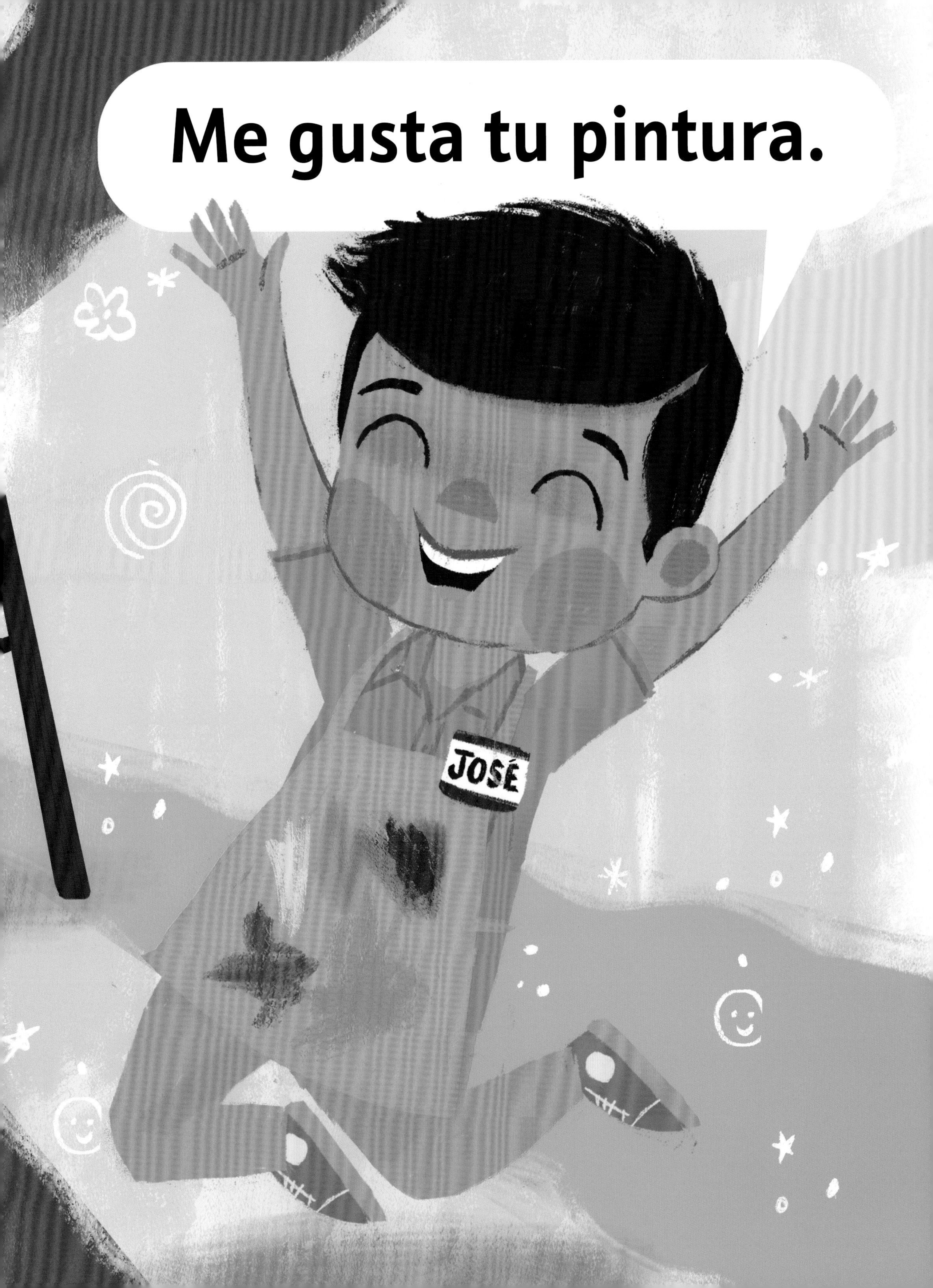
Me gusta tu pintura.
JOSÉ

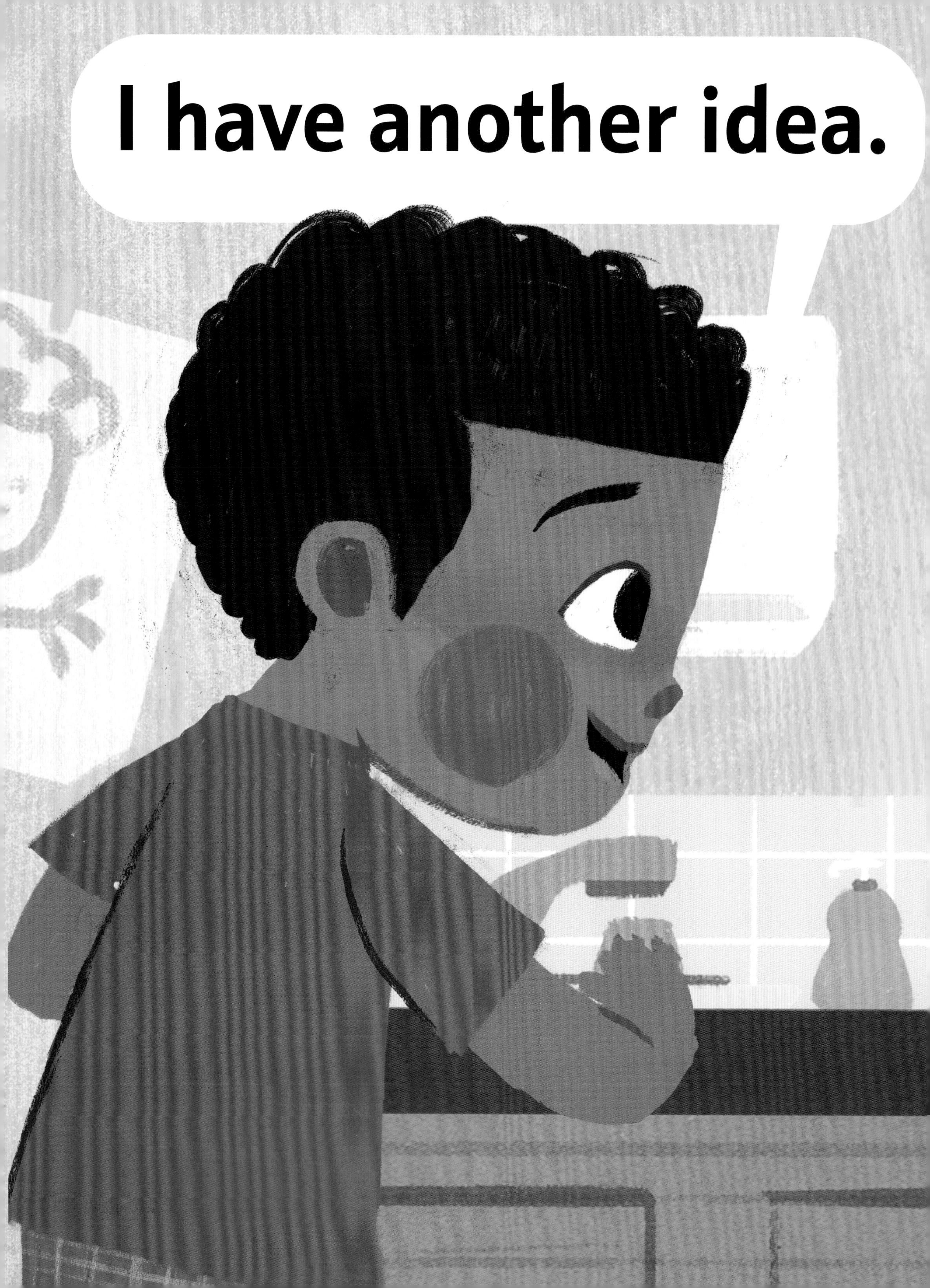
I have another idea.

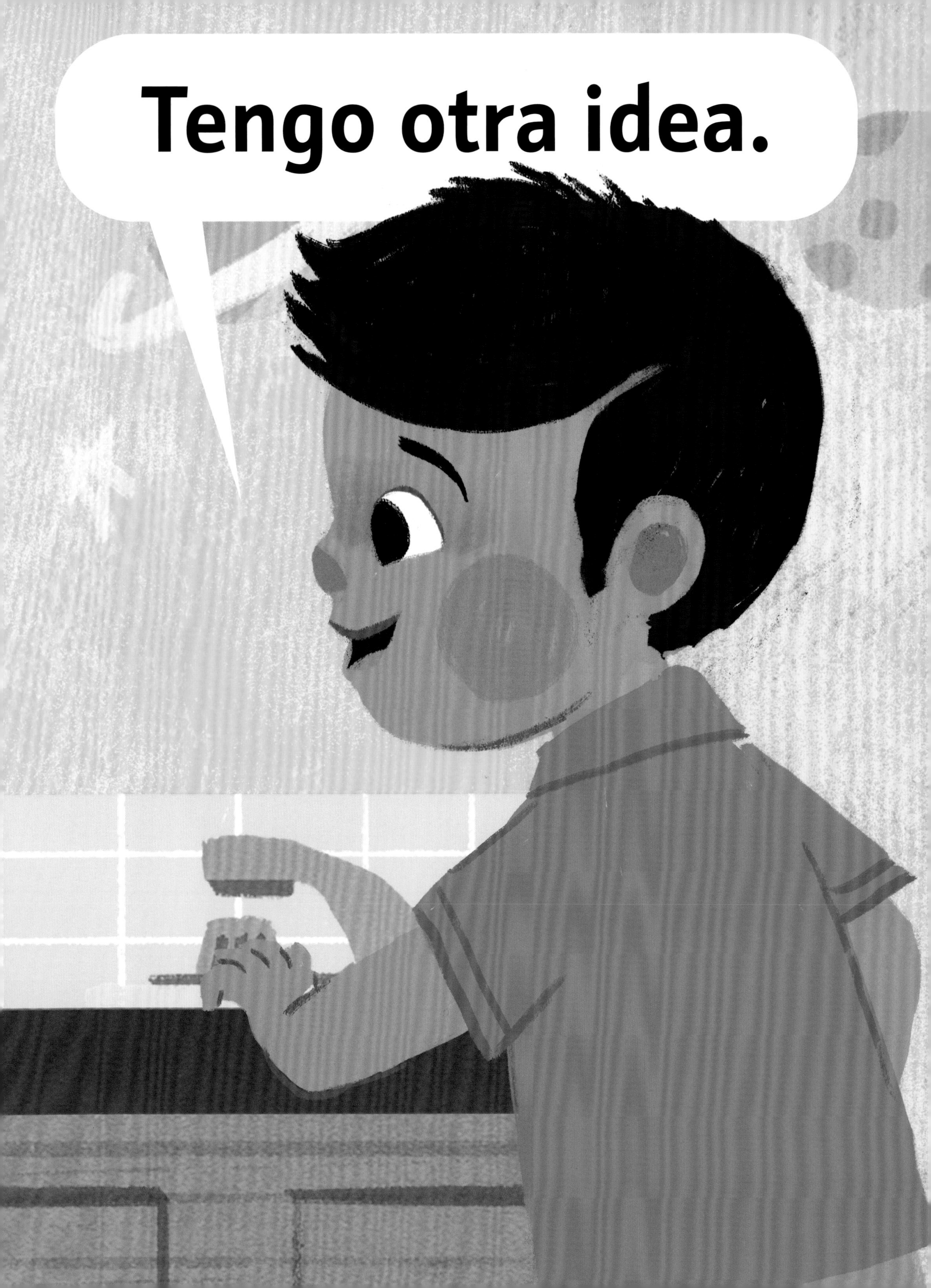
Tengo otra idea.

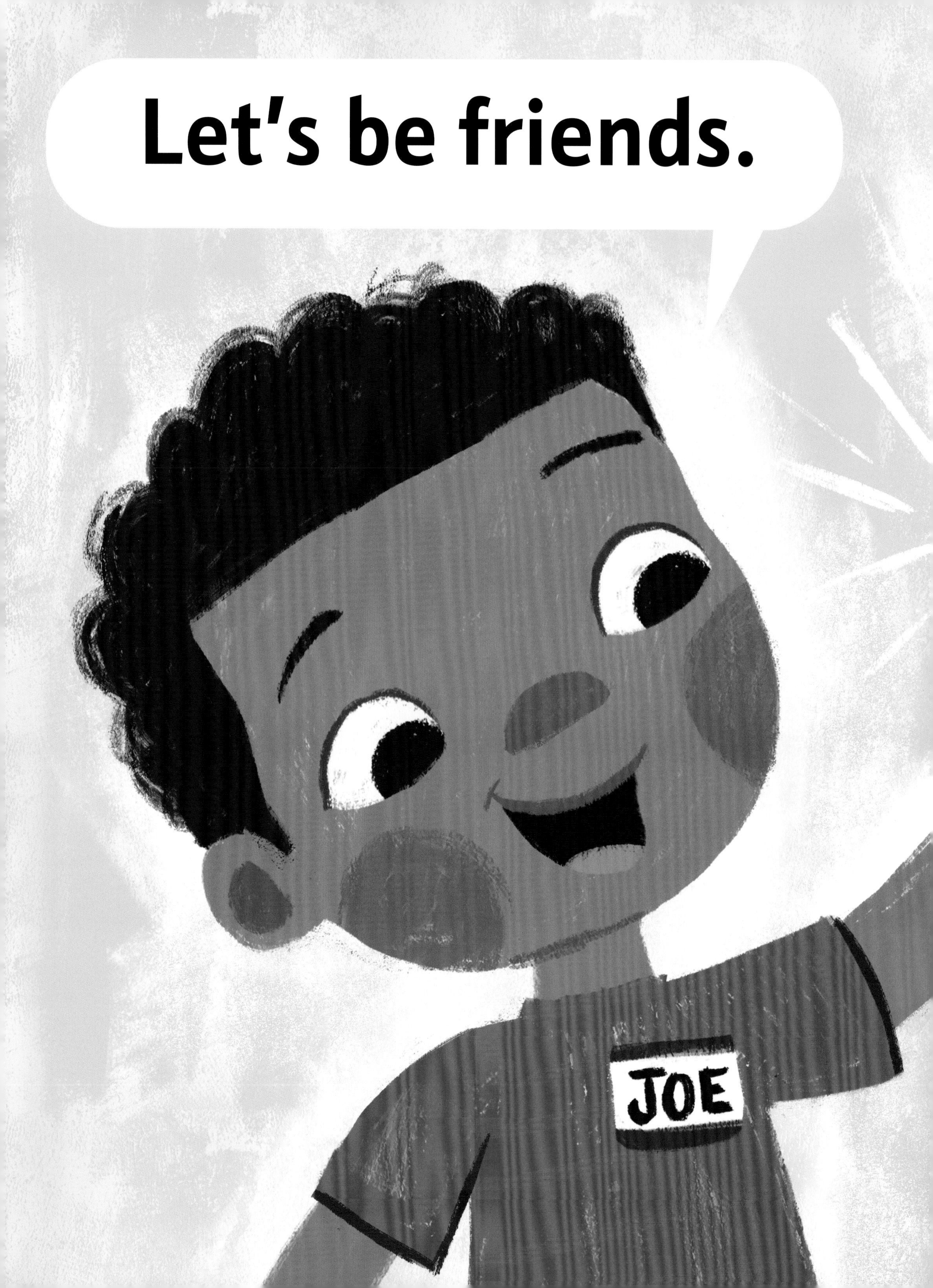
Let's be friends.
JOE

Words: Palabras

hi: hola

name: nombre

idea: idea

yes: sí

the colors: los colores

yellow: amarillo

blue: azul

green: verde

red: rojo

sun: sol

sky: cielo

house: casa

flowers: flores

painting: pintura

friends: amigos